CHOOSE YOUR OWN ADVENTURE®

Kids Love Reading
Choose Your Own Adventure®!

"I like the way you can choose the way
the story goes."
Beckett Kahn, age 7

"If you don't read this book, you'll get payback."
Amy Cook, age 8½

"I thought this book was funny.
I think younger and older kids will like it."
Tessa Jernigan, age 6½

"This is fun reading. Once you go in to have an
adventure, you may never come out."
Jude Fidel, age 7

Illustrated by Keith Newton
Book design by Stacey Boyd, Big Eyedea Visual Design
For information regarding permission, write to:

CHOOSECO
P.O. Box 46
Waitsfield, Vermont 05673
www.cyoa.com

A DRAGONLARK BOOK
ISBN: 1-933390-90-5
EAN: 978-1-933390-90-1

Published simultaneously in the United States and Canada

Printed in China.

0 9 8 7 6 5 4 3

CHOOSE YOUR OWN ADVENTURE®

YOUR GRANDPARENTS ARE ZOMBIES!

BY ANSON MONTGOMERY

A DRAGONLARK BOOK

*This book is dedicated to loving grandparents everywhere
(both zombie and nonzombie), but especially to Chini,
Shanny, Annie, Nana, and Boca.*

READ THIS FIRST!!!

WATCH OUT!
THIS BOOK IS DIFFERENT
from every book you've ever read.

Do not read this book from the first page
through to the last page.
Instead, start on page 1 and read until you
come to your first choice. Then turn to the
page shown and see what happens.

When you come to the end of a story,
you can go back and start again.
Every choice leads to a new adventure.

Good luck!

You wake up on a Saturday morning. Instead of watching cartoons or playing outside, you decide to make a potion. A zombie potion! With a zombie potion, people will do whatever you say. And you know just the people to use it on. Your grandparents!

Making a zombie potion is difficult. The list of ingredients is long, and some are hard to find. Getting a cat's hair ball is pretty easy. You just follow your grandparents' cat, Petey, around until he coughs up a nice juicy one. You check the list.

"Grandpa, do you know where I can find a snake's hiss?" you ask. He is eating eggs and toast. Your Grandma is making orange juice.

"I saw a garter snake sunning itself at the end of the driveway. Try there," he says, scooping a wiggly bit of egg onto his fork.

"Can we go to the fair today? Or maybe to the movies?" you ask.

Turn to the next page.

It's a test. You know the answer.

"Sorry, pumpkin, but we have to clean the basement and spread mulch on the garden. You can help!" your grandpa says.

"My friend Sally said you can see the whole town from the top of the Ferris wheel," you say. "And my friend Malik went to the movie theater with his dad and saw *The Floating Eyeball*. He said it's scary-silly, not scary-scary."

"Sorry, sweetie, but not today!" Grandma says.

"I'm going to look for the snake's hiss," you say, disappointed.

You find the snake. It makes a sound as it hides under its rock. You trap the hiss in your empty jar just in time. Then you get out of there, in case the snake gets mad.

Turn to page 5.

Making the rest of the potion is easier. You add some red bug juice, dirt, grass, leaves, and three winks. Now it is ready.

"Drink your orange juice, sweets," Grandma says when you come back into the house with your finished potion.

"Please can we go to the fair or the movies?" you ask Grandma. It's another test. "They have the shoot the clown balloon game at the fair, and you love movie theater popcorn, Grandma."

"No, dear," she says, smiling, "we have to turn over the garden and rake the front yard. Would you like to help?"

"Sure," you say, "if you take a sip of my zombie potion."

You smile your best innocent smile.

"Do pretend sips count with zombie potion?" she asks, looking at a piece of dirt floating on top with grass attached.

"Yes, I think so," you reply.

Turn to the next page.

She takes a pretend sip, and her eyes go blank. Your grandmother holds the jar out to your grandfather and says in a very zombie-sounding voice:

"Honey, try the lovely zombie potion our sweet grandchild has made for us."

"Okay, whatever it takes to get the mulch spread!" Grandpa says. He takes a REAL sip. And it is a big one.

Grandpa looks up at you and his eyes have gone blank too.

"What do you want to do?" he asks, shuffling to his feet. "We will do whatever you want!"

If you decide to go to the scary movie and get some popcorn, turn to page 9.

If you decide to go to the fair to ride rides and play games, turn to page 17.

"Let's go see a SCARY MOVIE!" you say, jumping in the air.

"Go fishing?" says Zombie Grandpa.

"Let's do both!" you yell, jumping up and scaring Petey the cat.

"I will get rods and worms," Zombie Grandma says, shuffling to get them.

"I will get the car," Zombie Grandpa says.

Turn to the next page.

You put a plate on top of the zombie potion and put a sticky note with a warning:
DON'T DRINK! ZOMBIE POTION!

There, that should keep it safe from your brother and your sister.

Turn to page 14.

You look at your grandparents. Grandpa's hair is in a messy swirl. He is shuffling around the lobby talking to the cardboard cutouts of the actors and chewing on a pencil.

Grandma is mumbling to herself. She gets in line with a bunch of little kids who are here for the little kids' movie. They don't run, but they move away from her fast!

Perfect! Your Grandparents ARE Zombies! You'll win the Scary Monster Costume Parade for sure.

The usher takes your arm and leads you into a big room.

The big room is filled with lots of people dressed up. You see aliens, cowboys, princesses, superheroes, and astronauts. But most are dressed as scary monsters. There are werewolves, witches, ghosts, goblins, and skeletons. They rub elbow bones with trolls, ogres, dragons, and vampires.

Turn to the next page.

But everyone stops what they are doing when they see your zombie grandparents!

"Unnghhhh…where is restroom…" Zombie Grandpa says, stumbling into a woman dressed as a giant squid.

"Get away from me!" she shrieks. One of her tentacles gets stuck on Zombie Grandpa and it wiggles over his head as he shuffles backwards.

CRASH! He bumps into Zombie Grandma and her face goes splashing into a bowl of purple punch.

Go on to the next page.

They are a complete mess. Perfect!

The judges are heading your way. You look at your zombie grandparents—but they're just standing up straight and acting normal!

The potion has worn off!

Your grandpa has straightened his hair, and your grandma has a bright-eyed smile. They're just your grandparents, and they're almost normal looking. The only prize you get is a coupon "For One Small Beverage of Your Choice!" that everyone gets just for being in the parade.

"Enough fooling around! It's time to go home," Grandma says. "There's mulching to be done!"

The End

14

"Wa-hoo!" you shout as you drive to the movie theater. You stick your head out of the window and open your mouth like a dog.

"Can we see the scary movie?" you ask, pulling your head back inside the car.

"Unngggggnnnnnnnnnnn…" Zombie Grandpa says as he slumps behind the wheel of his big car. It was bought before your dad and mom were born! That's how old it is.

"Turn left on…uggghhhhh…expressway… ugghhghhhhhh…south…" Zombie Grandma says, with long pauses.

Zombie Grandpa turns right instead of left, but you get to the movie theater after a little while.

You and Zombie Grandma get out, and Zombie Grandpa goes to park the car. You hear a loud CRASH from the parking lot, but Zombie Grandpa comes shuffling up to the front soon after. He drags his left foot but does not say anything.

Turn to page 16.

16

You walk in the doors of the movie theater, and you are amazed at how many people are here. There is hardly any room to move around. The popcorn makes your mouth water, and seeing the candy makes your stomach grumble.

"What should we see?" you ask Zombie Grandma. She has her glasses on and is peering up at the show listings.

"Maybe *Iguana Boy and the Flying Tarantula People, Part Two, Spread the Web?*" she reads.

"Hmm…" you think, but then someone interrupts you.

"Are you here for the Scary Monster Costume Parade?" a movie theater usher dressed in red with a cap on his head asks you. "There's a prize!"

If you say "yes" and enter the Scary Monster Costume Parade, turn to page 11.

If you say "no" and get some popcorn and see a movie, turn to page 18.

"We go to fair, we go to fair!" Zombie Grandpa says, shuffling out the door. Scrambled egg falls from his shirt to the floor. Petey the cat zips forward and gobbles it up. Then he scoots to freedom through the open door.

"Follow him!" Zombie Grandma says to you as she stumbles after them both. You aren't supposed to let Petey out. He gets lost. A lot.

"Wait for me!" you yell, running after your zombie grandparents. This could get out of control, you think.

Turn to page 21.

"Let's get some popcorn and see the show!"
you say. You lead your zombie grandparents
over to the concession stand.

"The big bucket of popcorn, with lots of
butter…" you say, but Zombie Grandpa
interrupts you.

"No butter…not good for…unnnhhhhnnn…
cholesterol…" he says, drooling a little.

"Umm, and a small, no butter, please," you
finish, handing over the money.

You can't believe that your grandparents are
actually taking you to see a scary movie! Your
friend Malik said *The Floating Eyeball* is super-
gross and scary!

Turn to page 26.

The fair is walking distance. But it takes a while to get there. Your grandparents are even slower as zombies than they were before. By the time you get there, you are really tired and thirsty.

"Lemonade...unngggggghhhhhh...please," Zombie Grandma tells the woman behind the lemonade stand.

The sun is hot, and the lemonade is refreshing.

"Thank you, Zombie Grandma!"

"You're welcome...oooooorrrghhhh..." she says. "Now what do you want to do?"

Turn to the next page.

You tell Grandma you want to ride the Ferris wheel. The Ferris wheel is right ahead, and it is a lot bigger than you thought it would be. The top is WAY up there. You are a little scared, but it would be nice to tell Sally that you rode it, too.

You are about to get in line for the ride. As you do, a woman and her daughter pass, carrying a giant panda. You would really LOVE to bring in a giant stuffed panda to school.

If you decide to play carnival games and try to win the panda or something like it, turn to page 24.

If you decide to ride the Ferris wheel, turn to page 32.

You decide to play some carnival games for prizes. Zombie Grandpa keeps missing the basket in the shooting game. And Zombie Grandma squirts you with the water pistol instead of the clown that makes a balloon fill up and pop. But you have fun anyway.

Finally you manage to hook a rubber duck with a star on its belly at the next game.

"You win any small prize, kiddo," the man with spiky hair behind the counter says.

Turn to page 36.

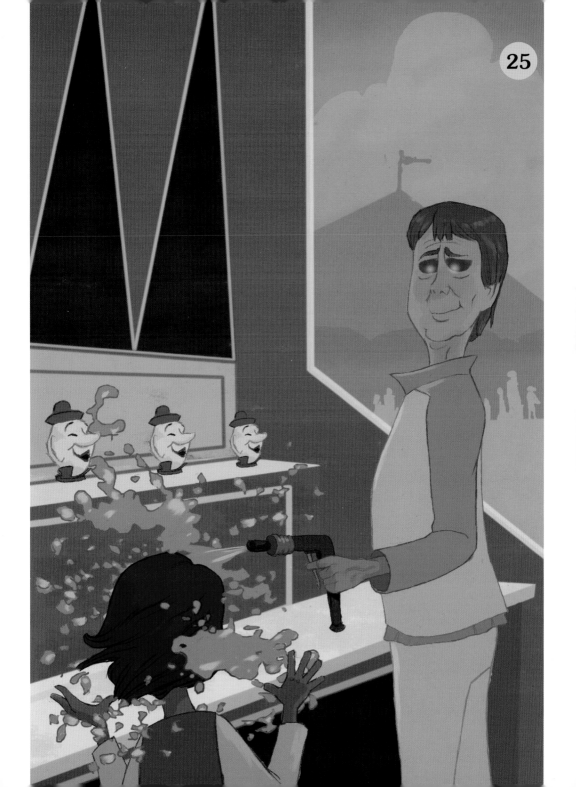

25

The theater is dark when you go in. It's hard to see, but every seat looks full. The previews are over, and the movie has already started.

Zombie Grandpa keeps moving in the dark theater, looking for a seat. He doesn't find any, so he goes down all the way to the front.

"Hey! Sit down!" someone yells as Zombie Grandpa goes from side to side looking for an empty seat.

He turns around just as the screen gets really bright. The light from the projector catches Zombie Grandpa's hair and makes it look freaky! Even worse, the floating eyeball in the movie floats RIGHT OVER GRANDPA'S HEAD. He looks like a monster!

"Oh my gosh! There's a zombie in here! A real one!" someone yells.

People start screaming. Then they run for the exits. Soon the whole theater is empty except for you and your zombie grandparents!

"See show...yeargghhhhhhhh!" Zombie Grandma says. She grabs a half-eaten Sugar Daddy off the floor and puts it in her mouth!

Zombie Grandpa picks up a tipped over bucket of popcorn and starts munching away.

You settle down in the empty theater and watch the movie. It isn't really scary, and it's sort of fun to be the only people watching.

The movie is almost over when the manager of the movie theater shows up followed by a scared-looking usher.

"I'm afraid you're going to have to leave," he says. His voice is trembling, and his flashlight shakes in his hand.

Turn to the next page.

"No zombies allowed in the theater. Except on screen, of course!"

"See end of eyeball movie…gurrggglleaaag-ggghh…" Zombie Grandma mutters, spraying bits of popcorn across the seat in front of her.

What should you do?

___

If you tell the manager that you just want to stay to see the end, go on to the next page.

If you tell the manager you will leave now, turn to page 44.

"See end of movie…arrhhhshhhehh… slurpp…" Zombie Grandma says, dribbling a bit of soda on her shirt. You have no idea where she found it.

"I'm sorry, but you really have to leave!" the manager says, trying to sound brave and forceful.

On screen, the eyeball is being taken captive by a band of brave heroes. It looks like the end of the movie is near. You decide to stall for Zombie Grandma's sake.

"Why do we have to leave?" you ask the manager. "We paid for our tickets."

Turn to page 50.

The line for the Ferris wheel is so long that you can't see the end of it. But when your zombie grandparents walk to the front, no one stops them from cutting the whole line.

You have to throw your tickets to the ticket taker because your grandparents brush right past and take a seat on the ride.

"Sorry!" you say.

There is room for six in the little swinging cage. But no one wants to ride with you and your zombie grandparents. So up you go by yourselves.

The view from the top of the Ferris wheel is beautiful. You can see every part of the fair. People are riding the roller coaster, eating candy apples, watching a pig race, and having a good time.

"Look, you can see your house!" you say to Zombie Grandma, pointing to the small yellow house in the distance. It looks so little from up here!

Turn to page 35.

"Go home?" Zombie Grandma asks, looking at you.

"Sure, we'll go home soon..." you answer, but before you can add "...but not yet," Zombie Grandma climbs out of the Ferris wheel cage, clambers down the side, and leaps into the ball pit next door. You see her struggle out of the ball pit and head toward home!

"Grandpa! What do we do? Grandma jumped off the Ferris wheel!"

He's asleep! He's snoring! And Zombie Grandma is running away!

The man opens the cage door, and you have to make a decision.

If you try and wake up Zombie Grandpa, turn to page 38.

Do you run after Zombie Grandma and leave Zombie Grandpa on the Ferris wheel? If so, turn to page 47.

You look at the stuffed animals and pick a parrot. It squawks, "Give me LOTSA crackers, buddy, SQUAWK! Goodbye!" when you squeeze it. It isn't giant, but at least you won something.

"I will get cotton candy…burrgggggg…" Zombie Grandpa mumbles as he stumbles away.

Turn to page 40.

"Wake up, Grandpa!" you shout, shaking his shoulder and yelling in his better ear. "Grandma is on the loose and heading for home. We have to catch her!"

Zombie Grandpa does not stir, but rather, he cuddles down in the corner of the cage and lets out a contented nap-time sigh.

"Uh, you gotta get out of the Ferris wheel, folks, people are waiting to get on," the ride operator says, tapping you gently on the shoulder. What do you do?

Then you have it!

"Grandpa, I think Grandma wants to go to the furniture store and buy all new furniture for the house!"

His eyes fly open and he sits straight up.

"Let's go get her!" he says. "I don't want her getting rid of my chair!"

Go on to the next page.

"Where did she go?" you ask the crowd. Everyone knows who you mean; they all point in the same direction.

Zombie Grandpa tears off after her, and you have to run to keep up with his long strides.

By the time you catch up with her, she is almost home, and the three of you walk the rest of the way in a tired silence.

Turn to page 51.

Zombie Grandpa lurches across the midway. People run out of his way. A little boy loses his balloon and starts to cry as it climbs into the sky.

"Cotton…unnggnnngnnnnnnnnnnnnn… CANDY!" Zombie Grandpa yells as he nears the cotton candy stand. The young woman working behind the counter looks up. At the sight of Zombie Grandpa, she backs away with her mouth hanging open.

With the cotton candy seller out of the way, Zombie Grandpa topples over the paper cones and puts both his hands into the machine!

When he pulls them out, he looks like he's wearing fluffy pink boxing gloves.

"Yum!" he says as he starts eating his candy hands.

"You look like you are eating a giant pink Q-tip, Grandpa!" you exclaim.

Turn to page 43.

"We better get him home," you say to Zombie Grandma. She nods and shuffles away to get the car.

Everyone is quiet during the car ride back. Grandpa is busy eating the cotton candy. Grandma mutters as she navigates traffic on the expressway.

Back at home, and weeks later, everyone pretends that nothing ever really happened on zombie potion day. No one mentions your trip to the fair, but there is still a HUGE sticky patch on the back seat of the car.

The End

"It's okay, Grandma," you say, patting her arm. "We'll go fishing instead! We already have the gear in the car!"

The theater manager and the ushers look relieved when you depart.

"All we need are worms!" you shout. Even though you did not get to see the end of the movie, you are glad to be out of the theater and in the sunshine!

Bill's Bait Shop is busy on this Saturday afternoon. They are having a contest for whoever can bring in the largest live catch. The top prize is $100!

Zombie Grandpa buys a fishing hat. You get a dozen Dilly worms. Zombie Grandma gets caught up in the fishing nets. But you straighten that out and go to the counter. Since you can't get them out, you do have to pay for the three orange fake worms that are stuck in Zombie Grandma's hair.

Turn to page 46.

The Fish Bowl is your favorite fishing spot. It's warm and sunny. You and your grandparents are the only people there.

"Grandma, can you help me bait my hook, please?" you ask politely. You really don't like putting the worm on the hook. It is so slimy and squiggly.

"Sure, dear…gagggggrrrrhh…dear, can you please hand me the worms?" Zombie Grandma says to Zombie Grandpa.

Turn to page 53.

"Grandpa, I'll be right back, I have to go get Grandma!" you shout as you dash out of the cage and after Zombie Grandma.

The fair is so crowded that you can't find her. You don't know what to do.

You are about to give up and go back to the Ferris wheel when you hear a loud roar of people shouting. Then they start running the other way.

"There's a zombie in the haunted house! She's eating everyone's candy!" a man with a floppy hat yells as he runs by.

It is hard going against the crowd. But you have to get to her before she gets in more trouble. You didn't think of these kinds of things when you were making the zombie potion.

You get to the haunted house. There is no one there when you arrive.

Turn to the next page.

"Grandma," you whisper into the darkness of the doorway. "I think you should come out and we should go on a different ride."

You look up at a big vampire painting above the door of the haunted house. He looks scary and mean. You have never been brave enough to go into the haunted house before.

"Unnggnnn...where's Grandma?...it's time to go home..." Zombie Grandpa says from right behind you.

You jump and give a little yelp. He snuck up on you!

Now you have to make a decision. Split up again, or team up to find Zombie Grandma?

If you choose to go into the haunted house with Zombie Grandpa, turn to page 52.

If you decide to have Zombie Grandpa wait at the exit, and you go into the haunted house on your own, turn to page 57.

49

"They are ZOMBIES!" he shouts, pointing at your grandparents.

"You don't have to yell. Look, they're helping you clean up!" you say, pointing to Zombie Grandma picking up a spilled bag of gummy worms. She pops them into her mouth, one by one.

"Please. Leave. Now." the manager says between clenched teeth.

"Sure," you say, standing up and looking back at the screen.

It says…

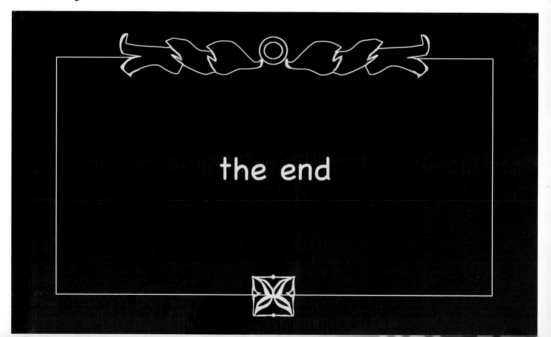

the end

At home, you have a wonderful afternoon playing with Petey, making bread, and working on your fort. By dinnertime, Zombie Grandma and Grandpa look like your regular grandparents. They tuck you in and read you a story and kiss you goodnight.

"We didn't spread any mulch today, Petey," you tell the cat snoozing on your pillow. He turns over and puts his paws in the air.

The End

"Come on, Grandpa. Help me find her," you say as you go into the haunted house.

It isn't that scary, just a bunch of things that make noise or jump out at you.

"Grandma!" you shout when you find her in the Monster Mash dance room. Wax figures of monsters are on the dance floor. Zombie Grandma is trying to talk to a wax zombie dancing with a werewolf.

"Well fine, have a good day!" she says, turning away from the wax zombie. "There you are, darlings, let's get out of this haunted house and into the sunlight."

"Yeah, it is probably time we get back to the house and finish the yard work," Grandpa says as you walk out of the haunted house.

You spend the rest of the day picking weeds, spreading mulch, and watering the plants. It isn't that bad, and it gives you time to think about how to make a werewolf potion…

The End

"Urgggggghhhh…" he says guiltily, and you look up from the hook.

He has opened the worms up, but instead of handing them to Zombie Grandma, he has one in his mouth! Yuck!

Turn to the next page.

"No, for the hook!" you say, lifting the hook up to show him. He nods and passes the worms to Zombie Grandma. She puts one on, and you lower the hook into the deep green pool of water.

ZING! Something grabs the hook and takes off! Your line spins until you start reeling it back in.

Both Zombie Grandma and Zombie Grandpa have to help you pull the fish in. It's a rainbow trout, and it's huge!

"Gasp! Gulp!" the fish says when you pull it up and get it in the net. It flips and twists in the net.

Go on to the next page.

"Cooonnnntessssttt? Unnnghhhhh…" Zombie Grandpa says, holding the container of worms. It looks like a bunch are missing, and there is some dirt on Zombie Grandpa's face.

Turn to the next page.

"I don't know," you say. "We just started fishing. Maybe we should just throw this one back and try for a bigger fish?"

The fish turns one eye to look at you.

If you choose to enter your fish in Bill's Bait Shop fishing contest, turn to page 60.

If you decide to throw the old rainbow trout back into the pond, turn to page 66.

You decide to go inside the haunted house alone. It is dark, and you're scared.

"Grandma?" you ask the darkness.

Suddenly a floating light starts moving past the cobwebs down the dusty hallway. You follow it.

A mummy jumps out of its sarcophagus, but you don't shriek. You are proud of that as you continue after the light.

Turn to the next page.

The dining room full of eating ghosts is more funny than scary. When they all look up and say "Boo!" you laugh.

Where is Zombie Grandma?

You are almost at the exit, when a hand reaches out of the darkness and grabs your arm. Is it the vampire from the picture?

"Time to go home, sweetie, don't you think?" Zombie Grandma says, smiling. You are a little scared, but a lot more happy to have found her.

"Yes, let's go home!" you say.

The End

"Grandma, grab the bucket! We have a prize-winning fish. We need to get to the bait shop!" you say, looking the fish in the eye. "Don't worry, buddy, we won't eat you. Besides, I think Grandpa likes the worms better anyway…"

Back at the bait shop, things are hectic. Guys pull up towing fancy bass boats with swivel chairs and stripes and sparkling paint jobs. The fish flops around in the bucket, but Zombie Grandma has a net on top, and she is making sure that he doesn't get out.

"Okay folks, Bobby Flambeau wins the prize for largest smallmouth bass. Three pounds! Give a hand to Bobby!"

"Thanks a lot folks; he was a fighter, but I got 'em!" Bobby says. He is almost as old as Grandpa, and he has on red overalls and he holds the fish up so everyone can see him.

Turn to page 62.

The crowd cheers.

"Next up, freshwater trout! Bring your catches up, and we'll weigh them," the announcer says.

Zombie Grandpa gives you a big thumbs-up as you take your fish up front.

You carry your trout in its bucket up in front of the crowd of people. Some people look at you and smile. Other contestants look nervous. Your fish is pretty big. The woman judging the contest takes your fish out to weigh it.

"Folks, we have a beautiful rainbow trout here. And it looks like a monster. The heaviest fish so far is two pounds, five ounces."

Your fish flops and wiggles, and the numbers on the digital scale go up and down and finally stop.

Go on to the next page.

"Too bad, but this one weighs two pounds, four and a half ounces," the woman announces. "Looks like you get second place, which entitles you to a $25 gift certificate to the bait shop!"

Oh well, second place is pretty good!

Turn to the next page.

Zombie Grandpa buys more worms with the gift certificate. You catch him opening the container a few times on the way to put the trout back in the lake, but you don't think he ate any more.

The fish seems to pause and stare at you with a mad look before it splashes its tail and heads to the bottom and out of sight.

"What a great day," you tell your zombie grandparents. Then you give them the biggest hug you can.

The End

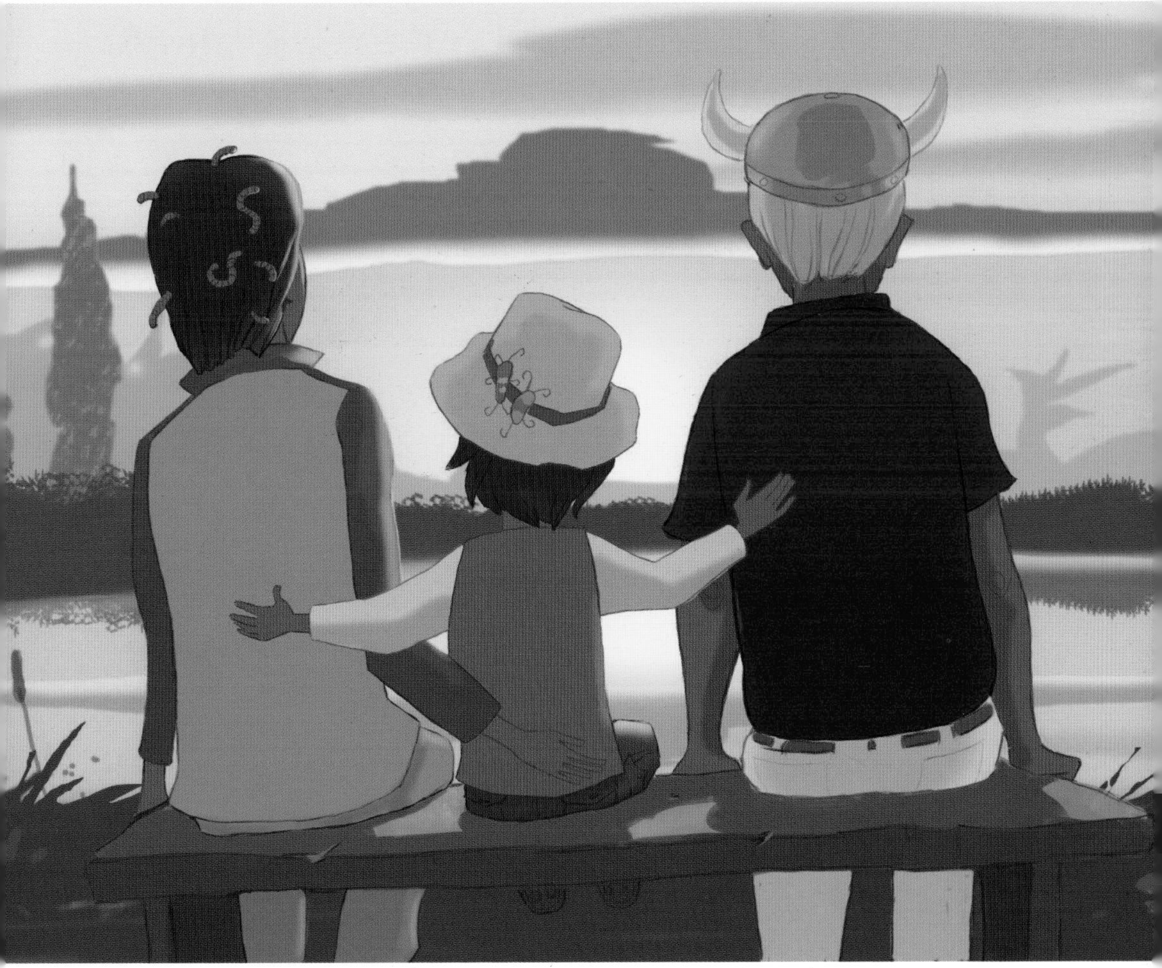

"He's pretty big," you say to Zombie Grandpa, trying not to disappoint him, "but I don't think he is going to win the contest. Why don't we just stay here and have a nice time?"

Zombie Grandpa looks disappointed. He grabs for the worms.

Go on to the next page.

"I bet you're tired," you say to Zombie Grandpa. "Why don't you take a nap?"

That's what he says to you when you're cranky, so you see if it'll work with him. You put the fish back in the Fish Bowl, and Zombie Grandma puts another worm on the hook. There are only two left!

Zombie Grandpa settles down for a nap. He puts his new fishing cap over his face and starts snoring immediately.

Turn to page 69.

The rest of the afternoon is wonderful. You catch and throw back a bunch more fish. Zombie Grandma falls into the Fish Bowl, but she manages to swim to shore and climb up the steep bank.

"You look more like a Fish Monster Grandma than a Zombie Grandma," you tell her when she gets out. Green lily pads hang down from her dripping hair, and she has a bullfrog on her head.

She doesn't smile, but she doesn't get mad. After she dries out in the sun, she gets you a sandwich and a drink.

Zombie Grandpa wakes up from his nap, and then you all go home.

"We're home!" you yell when you step through the kitchen door. But no one answers.

You freeze. Something is wrong, but you don't know what.

Turn to the next page.

Petey the cat comes up and gives you a snuggle. So he is fine. Then you see your older brother's backpack and your older sister's hockey bag.

Petey bats a crumpled bit of paper on the floor. It is your sticky note from before!

Then you look at the zombie potion. It is gone. Your brother and sister must have drank the potion.

Now you have a zombie brother and a zombie sister!

"Did you drink the zombie potion?" you ask, a little worried.

"Go to rock concert…ungggrhhhhh…need money for tickets…" your zombie brother says, shambling into the kitchen. "Need to sleep… need to eat…" He throws his backpack across the room and opens the fridge door. "Arrrrhhh-hhhhh…cooold…"

Turn to page 72.

72

You look over at your zombie sister. She is wandering in circles in the living room, looking down at her phone and texting while talking to herself.

"Go to mall...bblllarrhhhhhh...buy cleats for field...uunnghhhhhh...hockey...write paper... need sleep..." your zombie sister says.

Uh, oh. You know they are zombies, but will Mom and Dad be able to tell the difference when they come back?

The End

ABOUT THE AUTHOR

After graduating from Williams College with a degree specialization in ancient history, **Anson Montgomery** spent ten years founding and working in technology-related companies, as well as working as a freelance journalist for financial and local publications. He is the author of four books in the original *Choose Your Own Adventure* series, *Everest Adventure, Snowboard Racer, Moon Quest* (reissued in 2008 by Chooseco), and *CyberHacker* as well as two volumes of *Choose Your Own Adventure® The Golden Path*™, part of a three volume series. Anson lives in Warren, VT with his wife, Rebecca, and his two daughters, Avery and Lila.

ABOUT THE ARTIST

Illustrator: Keith Newton began his art career in the theater as a set painter. Having talent and a strong desire to paint portraits, he moved to New York and studied fine art at the Art Students League. Keith has won numerous awards in art such as The Grumbacher Gold Medallion and Salmagundi Award for Pastel. He soon began illustrating and was hired by Disney Feature Animation where he worked on such films as *Pocahontas* and *Mulan* as a background artist. Keith also designed color models for sculptures at Disney Animal Kingdom and has animated commercials for Euro Disney. Today, Keith Newton freelances from his home and teaches entertainment illustration at The College for Creative Studies in Detroit. He is married and has two daughters.

For games, activities and other fun stuff, or to write to Anson Montgomery, visit us online at www.cyoa.com

YOUR GRANDPARENTS ARE ZOMBIES!

BY ANSON MONTGOMERY

Have you ever read a book that's about *YOU?* This book is!

On a hot summer day, there are a lot of things you'd rather do than help your grandparents in the garden. What if you could make your grandparents do whatever YOU wanted? You have a zombie potion that will make you in control. Will your zombie grandparents behave when you take them to the fair, or to the movies? YOU choose what happens next!

Choose Your Own Adventure®
Dragonlarks *are an imprint of Chooseco LLC*

visit us online at cyoa.com